P9-CLS-912

Mouse & Mole

and the Christmas Walk

Printed in the United States of America.

Scientific American Books for Young Readers is an imprint of
W. H. Freeman and Company, 41 Madison Avenue, New York, NY 10010.

ISBN 0–7167–6560–8

10 9 8 7 6 5 4 3 2 1

For Kelsey and Jackie Williams

Mouse & Mole

and the Christmas Walk

by Doug Cushman

W. H. FREEMAN AND COMPANY NEW YORK

One winter morning Mouse appeared at Mole's front door.

"Look!" said Mouse. "It's snowing!"

"Wonderful," said Mole. "Especially since tomorrow is Christmas. I love a white Christmas."

"Me too," said Mouse.

"I am going into the woods today to pick out my Christmas tree," said Mole. "Would you like to help?"

"Sure!" said Mouse.

WINTER TIME!

Every year the Earth takes a trip through space around the sun. The whole time, the Earth is tilted.

When the part of the Earth where you live is tilted away from the sun,

it's winter.

The woods were covered with snow. They were very quiet.

"What kind of tree are you looking for?" asked Mouse.

"I'll know it when I see it," said Mole.

SNOWFLAKES
A snowflake is made up of many crystals (bits) of ice.
Some common snowflake shapes...
Star
Plate
Ice needle

The only sound that Mouse and Mole heard was the water in the stream running over the rocks.

"How about this tree?" asked Mouse.

"It's too tiny," said Mole.

"How about this tree?" asked Mouse.

"It's much too big," said Mole. "But we can use some of these pine cones for tree decorations." He stuffed them into his bag.

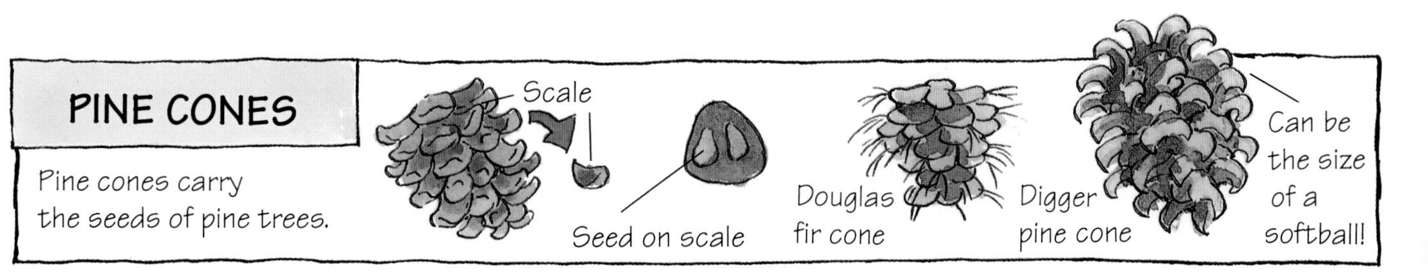

Then Mole saw a holly bush. Some of the leaves and berries were lying on the ground. He picked them up and put them into his bag.

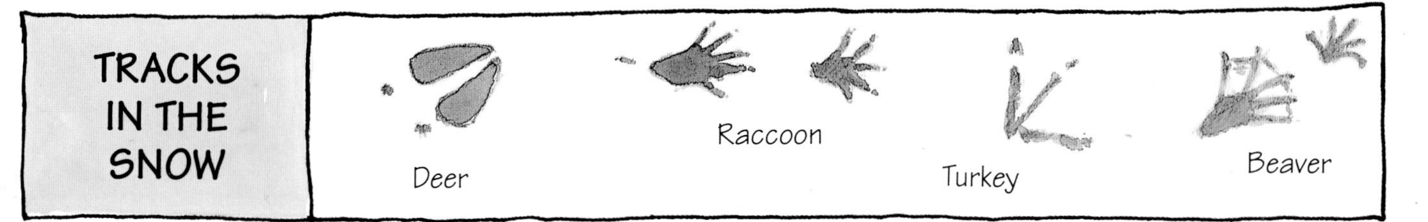
TRACKS IN THE SNOW
Deer
Raccoon
Turkey
Beaver

Mouse and Mole walked for a long time. Soon they came to a small clearing. In the center was a small evergreen tree.

Mole walked around it, looking at it from all sides. "I think this is the *perfect* tree," he said at last.

"Can we take it home now?" asked Mouse.

"No, not yet," said Mole. "Let's wait awhile. Then we can come back with the sled."

"I hate waiting," said Mouse. "What can we do until then?"

FOOD FOR THE WINTER

Food is hard to find in the winter. Squirrels eat buried acorns and nuts.

Woodpeckers hunt for insects.

Cottontail rabbits nibble on tree bark.

EVERGREENS
Evergreen trees are green all year round.
Evergreen branch
Evergreen leaves are called needles. They have a waxy coating to keep in water and help them stay green.

"We can borrow some skis," said Mole. "We can ski through the fields and look at the snow.

"Then we can build a snow fort and have a snowball fight."

"I hope I win!" said Mouse.

"Afterward we can go home and make a fire to get warm," said Mole.

"That would feel good," said Mouse.

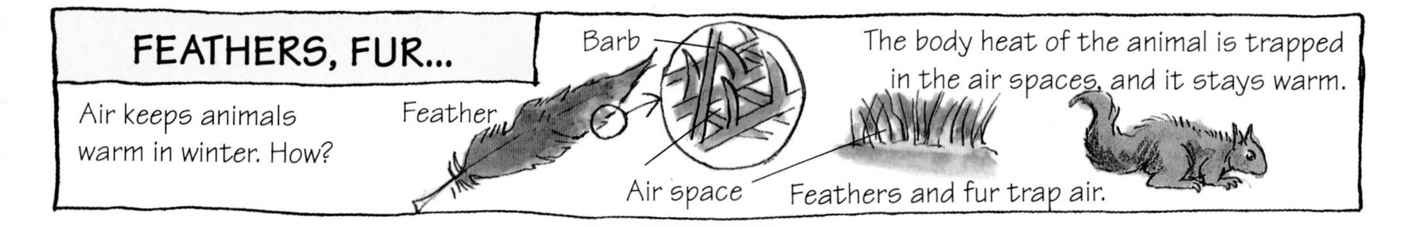

"Then we can go to the root cellar and get some vegetables from last summer's garden," said Mole. "We can make some hot soup."

"I love soup!" said Mouse.

"Finally, we can make hot chocolate to drink with some honey-spice cookies," said Mole.

And they did.

“That was delicious,” said Mouse. “*Now* can we get the tree?”

“Let’s make our decorations first,” said Mole.

Mole asked Mouse to pop some popcorn.
"Is this enough?" asked Mouse.
"I think so," said Mole.
They strung the popcorn on a long piece of thread.

Then they spread peanut butter on the pine cones and rolled them in birdseed. They tied a string around each one.

"I'm sure the birds will like these treats," said Mole.

"Birds?" said Mouse. "Did you invite birds for Christmas?"

"Just wait and see," said Mole.

Mole tied some red string onto the holly leaves. Mouse baked a big cookie star.

"I think that is everything," said Mole.

"Can we get the tree now?" asked Mouse.

"I'm too tired from all this work," said Mole. "Come back tonight."

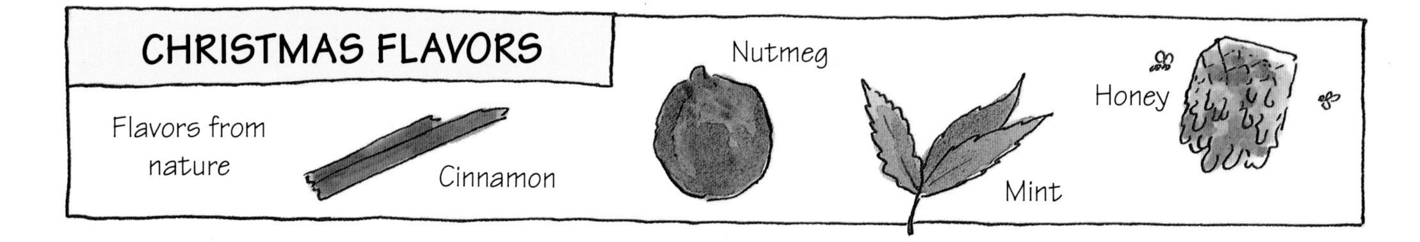

ICICLES
When water drips
from a rooftop...
0°C
32°C
if the temperature
is at the freezing
point of water
or below...
the drips freeze into icicles.

Mouse went home. He wrapped his Christmas present for Mole. Then he watered his plants and cleaned house. But it still wasn't nighttime.

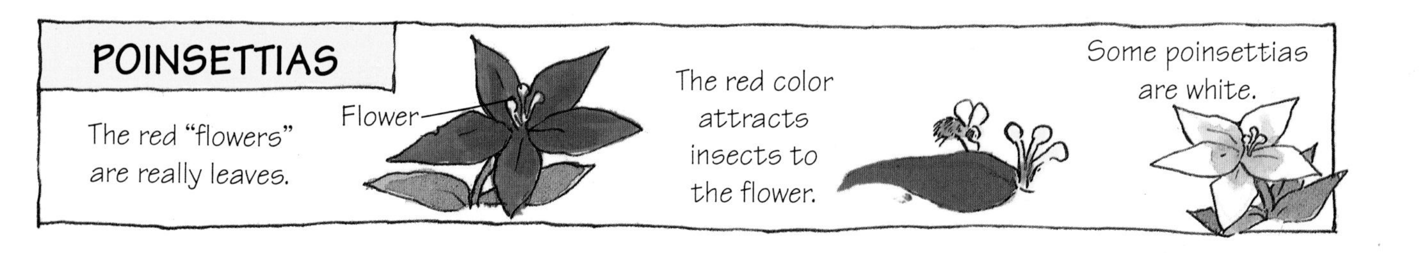

He looked out his frost-covered window until the sun went down.

"At last!" he said. "It is time to get the tree."

Mouse ran to Mole's house.
"I'm ready to get the tree," said Mouse.
"The sled is ready too," said Mole.
"Why are you bringing the decorations?" asked Mouse.
"You'll see," said Mole. "Let's go!"

LONG WINTER NIGHTS

Because the part of the Earth where you live is tilted away from the sun in winter... the sun is lower in the sky.

Summer sun

Winter sun

The sun rises later and sets earlier. The days are short, the nights long.

COLD WINTER NIGHTS
Because the winter sun is low in the sky...
the rocks and soil do not get as much heat from the sun.
And they have longer to cool off during winter nights.

THE MOON
The moon is our closest neighbor in space.
On the moon there are many craters (holes) and mountains.
There is no air or water on the moon.

The stars were bright in the clear night sky. The full moon made the woods very bright. Mouse and Mole found their tree.

"Can we take it home now?" asked Mouse.

"This is a wonderful tree," said Mole. "I think we should decorate it and leave it for all the birds to enjoy. It will make a nice Christmas present for them."

And that is what they did.
Mouse put the star on the very top.

STARS

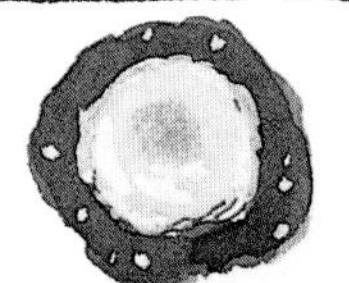

Stars are huge balls of hot gases far away in space.

They are made when dust and gases in space are pulled together.

Our sun is a star. It looks much bigger than other stars because it is much closer to us.

Back at Mole's house, Mouse and Mole opened their presents.

"Just what I wanted!" each one said.

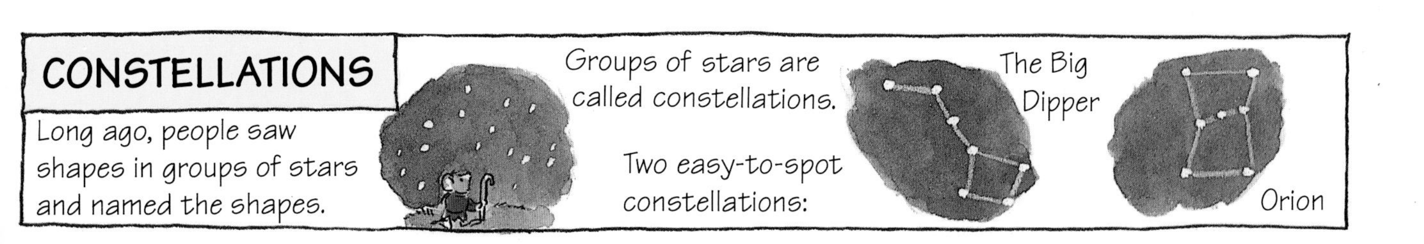

Early Christmas morning Mouse and Mole visited their Christmas tree. They watched the birds eating the decorations and tugging at the string. Mouse and Mole smiled at the happy birds.

"Merry Christmas, birds!" said Mole.

"Merry Christmas!" said Mouse.